It's MY Room!

It's MY Room!

by
Robert Munsch

illustrated by
Michael Martchenko

Scholastic Canada Ltd.
Toronto   New York   London Auckland Sydney
Mexico City New Delhi Hong Kong Buenos Aires

Scholastic Canada Ltd.
604 King Street West, Toronto, Ontario M5V 1E1, Canada

Scholastic Inc.
557 Broadway, New York, NY 10012, USA

Scholastic Australia Pty Limited
PO Box 579, Gosford, NSW 2250, Australia

Scholastic New Zealand Limited
Private Bag 94407, Botany, Manukau 2163, New Zealand

Scholastic Children's Books
Euston House, 24 Eversholt Street, London NW1 1DB, UK

www.scholastic.ca

The illustrations in this book were painted in watercolour
on illustration board.
The type is set in 19 point Lucida Bright.

Library and Archives Canada Cataloguing in Publication
Munsch, Robert N., 1945-
It's my room / Robert Munsch ; illustrated by Michael Martchenko.
ISBN 978-1-4431-1365-6
I. Martchenko, Michael II. Title.
PS8576.U575I88 2012a   C813'.54   C2011-906211-9

6 5 4   Printed in Malaysia 108   16 17 18 19 20

For Matthew White,
Fort McMurray, Alberta.
— R.M.

"LOOK!" said Matthew's mom. "We're going to have a big new trailer! You get your OWN room!"

"Well," said Matthew, "will there be lots of people in my room like in our old trailer?"

"NO!" said his mother.

"Well," said Matthew, "will there be just me in my room?"

"YES!" said his mother.

"YES, YES, YES, YES, YES!" said Matthew.

"How about dogs and cats and horses?" said Matthew.

"NO!" said his mother. "There will not be dogs and cats and horses. This is a room just for you and for you alone."

"YES, YES, YES, YES, YES!" said Matthew.

That day Matthew and his mom
moved into the new trailer.

"**WOW!**" yelled Matthew.
"Finally a room just for me!"

9

But the next day his mother said, "My brother from back home, the one with the two sons, is thinking of moving here and they will be visiting for a while."

"NO!" yelled Matthew. "NO! NO! NO! NO! NO!"

"Come on," said his mom. "It will just be for a little while."

So the two cousins came to sleep in Matthew's bed. It took Matthew a week before he could sleep without dreaming about stinky toes.

A week later his mother said, "Oh, Matthew, my sister is going to move here and her dogs are going to have to stay in your room for a while."

"NO!" yelled Matthew. "NO! NO! NO! NO! NO! Those are the dogs that ate the mailman and they will probably eat me while I am asleep."

"Nobody liked that mailman," said his mother, "and my sister needs help, so you will have to share for just a little bit."

So the two dogs came and slept in Matthew's bed. It took him a week before he could sleep without dreaming that he was being eaten by large, ugly dogs.

A few weeks later his mother said, "My five cousins are moving here, and they are bringing bunk beds, and they will be in your room for just a while."

"NO!" yelled Matthew. "NO! NO! NO! NO! NO! They all snore and I do not want them in my room."

"HA!" said his mother. "YOU snore, and they are my cousins, and that's that."

Matthew decided to sleep under the trailer. But mosquitoes and blackflies came out and almost ate him alive.

"I have had it!" said Matthew. "It is *my* room and not a hotel."

Matthew went into the trailer and took a package of pork chops out of the refrigerator. Then he walked down the road, past the trucks, to the dump.

21

At the dump he yelled, "Yo, bears! PORK CHOPS!"

Three bears followed Matthew. He ran back home, opened the door, and threw in the pork chops. The bears ran in after the pork chops.

Matthew's relatives yelled:

"BEARS!
AHHHHHHHHHHHHH!"

26

and they all ran out of the trailer and didn't come back.

When Matthew's mother got back, she was happy to hear that the relatives had left, so Matthew decided not to tell her that he was now sleeping with . . .

…bears.